Little Owl's Bedtime

For Rebecca and Joshua, with all my love —D. G.

For Auntie Barbara, one of the Bangor Night Owls! xx —A. B.

BLOOMSBURY CHILDREN'S BOOKS
Bloomsbury Publishing Inc., part of Bloomsbury Publishing Plc
1385 Broadway, New York, NY 10018

BLOOMSBURY, BLOOMSBURY CHILDREN'S BOOKS, and the Diana logo are trademarks of Bloomsbury Publishing Plc

First published in Great Britain in January 2020 by Bloomsbury Publishing Plc
Published in the United States of America in October 2020
by Bloomsbury Children's Books

Text copyright © 2020 by Debi Gliori
Illustrations copyright © 2020 by Alison Brown

Bloomsbury books may be purchased for business or promotional use. For information on bulk purchases please contact Macmillan Corporate and Premium Sales Department at specialmarkets@macmillan.com

Library of Congress Cataloging-in-Publication Data
available upon request
ISBN 978-1-5476-0449-4 (hardcover) · ISBN 978-1-5476-0450-0 (e-book) · ISBN 978-1-5476-0451-7 (e-PDF)

Art created with acrylic paint and colored pencil
Typeset in Mrs Eaves and Duper Pro
Book design by Kristina Coates
Printed in China by Leo Paper Products, Heshan, Guangdong
2 4 6 8 10 9 7 5 3 1

All papers used by Bloomsbury Publishing Plc are natural, recyclable products made from wood grown in well-managed forests. The manufacturing processes conform to the environmental regulations of the country of origin.

To find out more about our authors and books visit www.bloomsbury.com and sign up for our newsletters.

Little Owl's Bedtime

Debi Gliori

illustrated by

Alison Brown

BLOOMSBURY
CHILDREN'S BOOKS

NEW YORK   LONDON   OXFORD   NEW DELHI   SYDNEY

Little Owl was snuggled up with Mommy Owl
sharing a bedtime story. It was late o'clock.

"Then all the little bunnies closed their eyes and
fell fast asleep. The end," said Mommy. "Now it's your
turn, Little Owl. Close your eyes and . . ."

"NO," said Little Owl.

"NO,

NO,

NO!"

"No?" said Mommy Owl.

"NO," said Little Owl. "I don't want to close my eyes. I don't want to fall asleep. I don't want The End. I want another story."

Mommy Owl blinked. "If I read you one more story," she said, "promise me you'll snuggle down and go to sleep. It is VERY late for little owls."

Little Owl nodded.

Mommy Owl read Little Owl another story.

"Then all the little field mice closed their eyes and fell fast asleep. The end. Goodnight, Little Owl," Mommy whispered. "Sweet dreams."

"Sweet dreams," said Little Owl.

But . . .

Little Owl's pillow
was too lumpy.

Little Owl's quilt
was too hot.

Little Owl's eyes
refused to stay shut.

It was very dark.

"Mommy?" Little Owl called.

"Oh, Little Owl," said Mommy Owl.
"It has to be dark so that nobody can see
the very shy frogs when they come out
to sing in the Bashful Frog Chorus."

"I can't hear them,"
said Little Owl.

"That's probably because
they're very shy," said
Mommy Owl.

"Look, here's a tiny
night-light for you. It's so
small even a very shy frog
wouldn't mind you using it.
Goodnight, Little Owl."

Little Owl closed his eyes. His pillow was even lumpier than before. Little Owl wriggled and squirmed.

Suddenly Little Owl had an awful thought. "MOMMY!" he called. "I've lost Hedge, and I can't sleep without her!"

"Oh, Little Owl," sighed Mommy.
"Hedge has probably gone to pick up a
midnight snack at the Acorn Bakery."

"Found her!" said Little Owl.
"Look, she was hiding under my pillow."
"Phew!" said Mommy. "GoodNIGHT,
Little Owl."

"And Hedge," said Little Owl.
"Night, night, Hedge," said Mommy Owl.
"Now both of you—Go. To. Sleep."

Hedge fell asleep at once. Little Owl tried to go to sleep.
He tried REALLY hard. But there was a noise.

"MOMMY!"

"What's that n-n-noise?" squeaked Little Owl.

Mommy listened. "Is that the song of the bashful frogs?"

"No," said Little Owl. "It's a sort of quiet, snorty kind of noise."

"Oh, Little Owl," whispered Mommy Owl, "I know
exactly what that is . . ."

"It's the sound
of little butterflies
snoring in their flower
beds. So sweet. We're
so lucky to hear them."

"Goodnight, Little Owl,"
said Mommy Owl again.
And all was quiet until . . .

"MOMMY!" called Little Owl.

"I'M TOO HOT.

I'M HUNGRY.

"I GOT TO GO P—"

"Oh, LITTLE OWL,"
said Mommy.

"Look, you've woken up
Hedge. Poor Hedge! Let's
tuck her back in."

"Mommy?" said Little Owl.

"Yes, Little Owl," sighed Mommy Owl.

"I can't fall asleep because I'm too excited about seeing Grandma and Grandpa Owl tomorrow."

"My dear Little Owl," said Mommy Owl.
"Shall I tell you a secret? Tomorrow will
come much faster when you fall asleep."

"Really?" Little Owl yawned.

"I promise," said Mommy.

"You forgot to give me a kiss," said Little Owl.

"Silly Mommy," said Mommy Owl. "Love you,
Little Owl."

"Love you, too, Mommy," said Little Owl.

Little Owl settled down with Hedge.

"I'll read you one more story, Hedge, but you have to promise to go to sleep afterward because the faster you go to sleep, the faster tomorrow will come. And tomorrow we're going to see Grandma Owl and Grandpa Owl."

Little Owl turned off his night-light.

"It is dark, but I'm right here beside you."

Little Owl tucked Hedge in.

"That sound? It's just Mommy Owl singing in the bath.
Night, night, Hedge, sleep tight."

Little Owl couldn't wait for tomorrow to begin.
He closed his eyes extra tight, pulled the quilt
up to his chin, and snuggled deep into his pillow
with a huge, happy yawn.

Mommy Owl tiptoed in for one last kiss.
"Sweet dreams, Little Owl."